THE
POTTER'S
FOUR
SONS

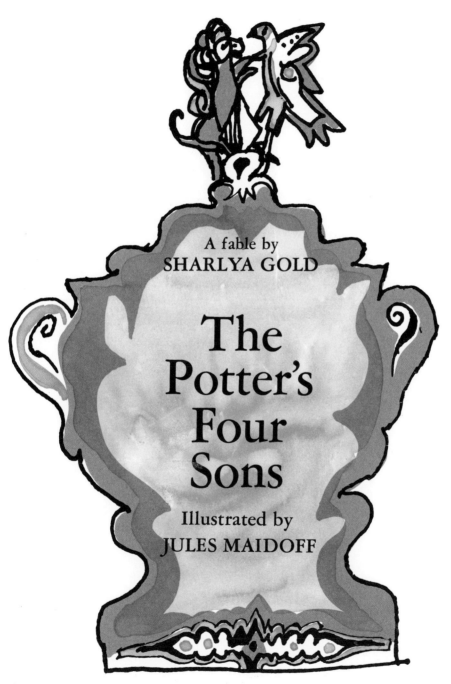

A fable by
SHARLYA GOLD

The Potter's Four Sons

Illustrated by
JULES MAIDOFF

Doubleday & Company, Inc. 1970

AUTHOR'S NOTE

Special words pertaining to holidays
and customs are defined in an illustrated
glossary at the end of the story.

S.G.

Copyright © 1969 by Sharlya Gold
Library of Congress Catalog Card Number AC 71-78723

To my uncles
Ozer, Al, and Simcha
whose kindness never failed me

Long ago in a small country lived an old Jewish man and his four sons. The father was a potter and made clay jugs, jars, bowls, and pots of every size and shape. He was neither rich nor poor but made a sufficient living.

The boys, Gershon, Haskell, Nabar, and Shimin, had doubts about following their father's trade. They had little interest in molding the wet clay and decorating the finished pots and jugs. They did whatever tasks their father asked, but without joy.

The old man felt very sad when he saw other fathers working side by side with their sons at the family trade. The tailor and his son sat cross-legged next to one another diligently stitching a new robe for the rabbi to wear on Rosh Hashana. The shoemaker's two sons cut and stitched leather while listening eagerly to their father's directions. Even the baker's small son helped sift flour for Friday's challah. With every contented father and son he saw together, the old man grew sadder and sadder.

One day he said to his sons, "I know that you do not wish to become potters and that in time you must lead your own lives, following the trade you love best. Tell me, what is it that you wish to do?"

The four sons looked at one another in wonder. Never had they considered what they *wanted* to do, but only what they didn't want to do.

Presently Gershon, the eldest, said, "I want to see something of the world. I don't want to spend my whole life in our small village."

Haskell, the second eldest, agreed. "It is not only that we do not wish to become potters. It is that we do not know what the world has to offer."

Nabar, the second youngest, nodded. "I have seen all the trades in our village, and yet I feel there must be many kinds of work I have never seen."

Shimin, the youngest, asked gently, "Father, is it wrong to feel thus?"

"No, it is not wrong to feel that the world has marvels you wish to see. Even I did not always want to be a potter like my father before me and his father before him."

He shuffled to the back of his shop and returned with four small clay pots filled halfway to the top with gold coins. He handed one pot to each of his sons. "Go where you will and learn what you wish. See everything until your eyes are weary of looking and your legs are weary of walking. Then come home and tell me what you have decided to do with your lives."

The four boys shouted for joy and hugged their father. When they were ready to go, Shimin asked solemnly, "Why did you give us pots for the gold instead of purses?"

The old man smiled. "I want you to remember wherever you carry these pots that you also carry your father's love." He patted Shimin's shoulder. "Some of you may come back with full pots and some with empty ones, but it does not matter. The coins are yours to use as you wish."

The four sons kissed their father good-by, agreeing to return at the first moon of the month of Kislev. They hurried along the road that led from their village until they came to a dividing point—four separate paths going in four different directions. There they parted with many hugs, handshakes, and good-luck wishes.

Gershon hurried along the first road to the left until he came to a town. He was eager to find a resting place for the night so that he might begin to see the comings and goings of the city. He stopped at the Lion of Judah, the first inn he saw, and made arrangements to sleep there. Then he wandered into the market place. He watched the many women who strolled from stall to stall, their arms filled to overflowing with their purchases. Gershon stopped at a stall and ordered some delicious-looking pancakes from the old woman who was making them. When he dipped his hand into his pot to take out a gold piece, the woman exclaimed, "What a fine pot! If we have some pots here, people could buy more pancakes to take to their families. As it is now, they buy only as many as they can carry in their hands. Will you sell me your wonderful pot?"

By this time many people were crowding around Gershon, shyly touching his earthenware pot. "I would like to buy it, too," said a woman with a circle of children pulling at her skirts. "Then I wouldn't have to fill my children's little arms with my purchases."

11

"I cannot sell you *this* pot," said Gershon, "but I will make others and sell them to you." The people shouted their agreement and followed him to the riverbank. They watched him dig the clay and shape it into pots. They watched him set the pots in the sun to dry and then put them into a heated-rock oven he had built. So many people came to buy that Gershon was busy every day. He made pots, jugs, jars, and bowls and sold all he made.

Suddenly one day he realized that it was almost the new moon of the month of Kislev. Time had slipped by, even though he had not seen and done everything he had planned.

"I must go," he told the people.

"But who will make pots for us?" they asked sadly. "Some of us have tried to make the jugs and jars, but no one can make them so well as you. If you only had a son who would carry on your trade!"

Gershon knew they were right. "Perhaps I shall come back again," he replied.

He said good-by to the landlord at the Lion of Judah, picked up the small pot his father had given him, and started homeward. He had received so many gold coins from the pots he had sold that his own overflowed. Gershon walked quickly. The thoughts of his father, his brothers, and his home made the long miles shorter.

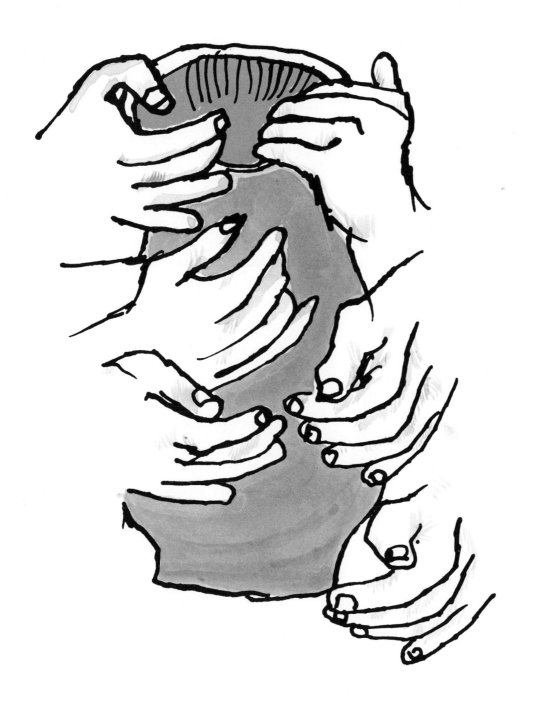

Haskell had chosen the road which disappeared over the hill. When he reached the city, he sought out the finest inn and ordered the very best food. Then he wandered down the Street of Entertainments, watching magic tricks and dancing girls and listening to the astronomers tell the wonders of the heavens. Each time he came to some new entertainment, he dipped freely into his pot of gold coins. But soon he grew alarmed. How quickly his pile of coins had dwindled! Only a few remained, clinking lonesomely against the bottom. "Tomorrow I must find work," he decided, "or else I must return home."

Early the next day he returned to the Street of Entertainments and asked for work. "Can you do magic tricks?" asked the magicians, pulling a silk handkerchief from Haskell's ear.

"Can you read the heavens?" asked the astronomers, looking for daytime stars with their telescopes.

"Can you teach new dances or sew costumes?" asked the owner of the theater where the dancing girls performed.

To all these questions Haskell said, "I only know how to make clay pots."

"Well, then," said the magicians, "by all means *make* clay pots. It doesn't matter what you do so long as you do it well."

Haskell finally found work with a potter, but to his amazement this potter made cups and plates from *colored* clay and printed his customers' names on them. He also made vases and ornamental bowls for flowers. Haskell grew more and more excited by all the wonderful things he was learning. He worked hard and well and tried to remember everything so that he could teach his father. He was so busy that he did not realize how quickly time had passed. It was almost the new moon of the month of Kislev. He asked for his wages and said that he must leave.

The potter was very sad, because Haskell had learned so quickly and had done such good work. "I have no sons," he said. "This business could be yours when I am too old to work."

Haskell thanked him and said, "I have a father of my own, but perhaps one day I shall come back." He placed his wages in the pot his father had given him and started out. The feel of the clay pot made him yearn for home, and he hurried to be on time.

When Nabar left his brothers, he hastened down the road with a glad heart. All his life he had wanted to try the different types of work in his small village, but he knew that each man had a son to learn the family trade. Nabar could not ask the tailor or the baker to teach him. How would it look if a son studied another man's trade? Nabar loved his father too much to embarrass him in the eyes of others.

The city to which Nabar was going was more than a day's journey. When night closed in, he found himself near a dark woods. From time to time he saw the glistening yellow-green eyes of a wild animal shine through the thick bushes. Thinking it would be better to stop and wait till morning, Nabar looked about him for shelter. He spied a tiny wooden hut thatched with twigs. "Perhaps I can stay there or at least buy a bit of dinner," he said to himself, dipping his hand into his pot of cool gold coins.

He strode toward the hut and knocked boldly. A rough-looking fellow opened the door and said with an unfriendly sneer, "What do you want?"

Nabar felt his own smile freeze. Suddenly he didn't feel so brave. He backed away and tried to cover the clay pot with the folds of his cloak. "Nothing," he said faintly. "I . . . knocked by mistake."

The man's crafty eyes were too quick. He had seen the clay pot and had heard the faint clink of coins. Immediately his mouth assumed a kind of smile, although his eyes remained cold.

"It's dark, and you must have traveled a long way. Are you going to Shevvat?"

"Yes," Nabar answered hesitantly.

The man opened the door wide. "Come in and rest awhile. Perhaps you would like something to eat."

Nabar looked longingly at the warm fire that crackled inside and sniffed hungrily at the smell of cooking food that drifted outside. He squeezed his arms more tightly about the clay pot. "Well . . ."

The man coaxed, "Perhaps you are shy because you have no money and cannot pay for your dinner. I do not care. I live a lonely life and am glad to have your company."

Nabar felt better. He decided that the man did not know about his gold. "All right," he agreed. "Thank you."

While his host busied himself dishing up the meal, Nabar removed his cloak and draped it about the pot, concealing it completely.

Soon Nabar felt very comfortable. The food had filled his empty stomach, and the fire was warm on his back. Almost before he knew it, his eyes were closing. Nabar struggled to stay awake. He studied his host, who was lying on a rough cloth near the fire. The man's eyes were shut, and he breathed heavily. "I shall nap for only a few minutes," Nabar decided, "and I shall be up and on my way before that fellow awakes. Even though he has shown me only kindness, there is something about him I do not trust. I would rather take my chances in the woods with the wild animals than spend the night with this scoundrel."

Nabar slept. He did not awaken until the thin fingers of golden sunlight nudged his closed eyelids. He sprang up at once and saw that he was alone. Even the fire had gone out, leaving a cheerless pile of ashes. His cloak was carelessly heaped on the floor, and the clay pot lay in a corner—empty! Nabar searched everywhere, but not a single gold coin could he find.

He sat still for a few moments, his head buried in his hands. Then he picked up his clay pot, shook out his dusty cloak, and set off again for the city. "I will work hard, save my wages, and refill my bowl with gold coins. When I return home at the appointed time, no one will guess that I have been robbed."

When Nabar arrived in the city, he went immediately to a bakery. "I want to learn your trade," he said.

"Let me see your arms," said the baker. "They must be strong to knead the dough."

As Nabar thrust out his arms he was suddenly glad that he had worked as a potter. His muscles were hard from pounding and shaping the clay in his father's shop.

The baker felt his firm muscles and looked at his strong hands. "Good. Have you made bread before?"

"No, but I am eager to begin."

Nabar was set to work kneading the dough. His arms ached as he pummeled the sticky mass, pounding in huge quantities of flour to make it smooth and elastic. Then he learned how to shape the loaves and let them rise until they were light. Finally he learned to put them into the oven on a long-handled, flat paddle and pull them out when they were crusty and brown. He worked very hard and even learned to bake cakes, cookies, and rolls.

All too soon it was time for Nabar to leave. The baker coaxed him to change his mind. "I will give you all my secret recipes. I have no sons to carry on for me, but my daughter Rachel is a lovely girl. Perhaps one day you and she . . ."

Nabar's face grew red. He knew how pretty Rachel was. Had they not smiled at one another whenever she came to the bakery? But he shook his head. "I promised to be home at the first new moon of the month of Kislev. But perhaps I shall return."

He received his wages from the baker and paid the master of the inn where he had stayed. Then he started for home with his clay pot tucked under his arm.

"It is true that my pot is empty," he thought to himself, "but my head is full of new ideas. I can bake bread that is fit for a king!"

Shimin had chosen the last road to the right, but he waved to his brothers until they were out of sight. Actually he didn't mind being a potter, and he was a little afraid of going off on his own. More than anything else Shimin liked to make up tales and daydream about people. Working with clay allowed him time to create stories about his father's customers.

Shimin decided to ask for work at the first potter's shop he saw. Later, when he knew his way about the strange city, he would try a different trade.

He was hired at once in a small shop on the outskirts of the city and accepted lodging with the potter's family. But soon he realized that the potter did not care at all about the pots made in his shop. The bottoms were often coarse and uneven. Sometimes small pebbles were left in the clay, so that the pots were easily broken. Often, too, there were air bubbles in the clay, and many pots exploded when they were fired.

When Shimin mentioned the poor quality of the pots, his employer raged at him. "I make what people buy! If they buy poor pots, I shall make poor ones. If they demand better pots, then better pots I shall make."

Shimin was not satisfied. His father had taught him always to do his best. He could never make poor pots on purpose!

Shimin decided to leave the potter and asked for his wages but the potter only laughed. "You have only been with me a short time. Your wages were used to pay for your meals and for your bed."

Shimin walked up and down the streets of the city, looking for another shop, but by nightfall he still had not found work. He had to dip into his precious pile of gold coins to buy food and lodging. In the morning he bought a simple breakfast and set out again.

On a narrow street lined with tumble-down houses, Shimin spied a tiny shop and asked for work. The potter shook his head. "I can barely feed myself. Those who buy from me have little money." He held out a coarse misshapen bowl and apologized. "I could buy finer clay, but then the bowls would cost more. My customers could not afford them at all."

Shimin thanked the old potter and set out again. All that day he found no work to his liking and had to dip again into his clay pot to buy dinner and lodging.

On the third day Shimin found a very large potter's shop. He watched the richly dressed customers go and come. He stared at the magnificent bowls they bought, bowls ornamented with emeralds, rubies, and diamonds.

Shimin longed to ask for employment there, but he knew nothing of such beautiful work. Finally, when his coins were gone, he approached the owner, a large, fat man who supervised the work and wore diamond rings on his soft, pudgy hands.

"I am looking for work," Shimin said shyly. "I can make bowls and pots, although I have never made any so beautiful as the ones I see here."

The owner looked at him shrewdly. "Do you have a sample of your work?"

Shimin held out his empty pot proudly. "My father made this. He is a fine potter and has passed his secrets on to me."

The fat man passed his hands carefully over the bowl and held it up to the light, looking for flaws. Satisfied at last he said suspiciously, "You say your father made this fine pot. If that is true, why are you not working in your father's business?"

Shimin swallowed hard, knowing his words would sound foolish. "I want to see a little more of the world before I settle down," he explained. The man laughed so heartily that all his stomachs jiggled. At last he wheezed, "So you think you will see more of the world from inside my shop?"

Only the thought of his empty clay pot kept Shimin from turning away.

At last the owner said, "You may work here. See to it that your pots are as good as your father's."

Shimin found the work difficult because his patrons were so quick to find fault. Often he had to remake a bowl to please a dissatisfied customer. And as he was paid only for completed work, on some days he received no money at all and went to bed hungry.

The young man found it increasingly difficult to make up stories about his customers. He was too tired most of the time to do anything but follow orders. Shimin longed for the time to pass quickly so that he could return home. At last it was almost the new moon of the month of Kislev, and he told his employer he had to leave.

The fat man stared at him for a moment and laughed. "Have you seen enough of the world already?" Then he frowned. "You have not yet completed that large, emerald-studded vase."

"Someone else can do it as well as I," replied Shimin, in a hurry to be away. "I have done half, and the one who completes it can keep my part of the money."

The owner agreed and asked, "Do you have enough money to reach home?"

Shimin shook his head. He had saved nothing. All had been spent just to maintain life. The fat man said quickly, "I will buy your clay pot, and you can buy provisions with the money. A good meal will put strength in your legs." He jingled a bag of coins. "Come, sell it to me."

Shimin hesitated. What would his father say? Suddenly his stomach rumbled hungrily, for he had eaten only bread for supper and nothing at all for breakfast. Shimin realized his father would rather have him alive and well than possess any number of clay pots.

He handed the man his bowl and received a handful of coins. Then he bought bread and cheese and started for home.

There was much laughter and rejoicing when the four brothers met at last at the crossroads. They agreed not to tell their adventures until they arrived home. As they hurried along the dusty road that led to their small village, each was silent, wrapped in his own thoughts. On every side the trees and bushes and bends in the road were familiar and heart-tugging. Suddenly, though not a word was spoken nor a glance exchanged, they began to run. They fairly flew, the dust swirling at their heels. Straight ahead was their home, and there, standing by the road, was their father! He was peering toward them, waving wildly.

What embracing, what love, what tears and laughter filled the air! Finally the old man seated himself on a small bench and the four boys crowded round, bombarding his ears with their adventures.

"Wait, wait." He smiled. "You are all talking at once. Let's go inside and have some hot tea. Then you shall tell me what wonders you have seen."

The boys gulped their tea impatiently, waiting for their father to finish. When the last drop was gone, he turned to the eldest. "Gershon, you begin."

Gershon proudly thrust out his pot. The heaped-up gold coins spilled from the top. "As you see, I have more than I began with." His father and brothers listened closely, their eyes round with wonder at the thought of a village that had never known pots or bowls. Finally Gershon said, "It is odd. Although I never before wanted to be a potter, now I think it is the best trade in the world." He smiled at his father. "And when I have a son, God willing, I shall want him to be a potter, too."

The old man nodded. "We understand one another better now, eh?" Then he turned to his next eldest. "Well, Haskell, what happened to you?"

Haskell set the clay pot, half-full of gold coins, on the table. "I, too, spent my time making pots and bowls." His eyes shone. "But, Father, I learned many new techniques. I know how to color clay and to fashion many objects of beauty."

His cheeks reddened. "But I did not intend to be a potter in that great city." His brothers nodded knowingly when he explained, "I could practice no new trade because no one was willing to teach me. Magicians only wanted to hire those who were already magicians, and astronomers were interested only in other astronomers."

The old father clapped his hand softly on Haskell's shoulder. "That is so. And as you found out, the potter who taught you so many things was interested only in another potter—not a magician or an astronomer."

Now it was Nabar's turn. "I have no profit like Gershon and Haskell —nor any coins at all. He set his empty bowl on the shelf and tried to smile. "At least you can sell my bowl, Father."

"Tell us of your adventures, my son," his father said. "Perhaps you have more profit than you know."

Nabar told of entering the man's hut, eating the stew, falling asleep, and awakening to find he had been robbed of his coins. His brothers listened wide-eyed. The only other sound was his father's occasional murmur, "A shame . . . a shame."

At the end of the story about the bakery Nabar said, "The baker has a daughter . . . she is very pretty . . . she likes me, I think." He swallowed with embarrassment. "The baker has no sons. He would like me to marry his daughter and become a baker, too."

Gershon slapped his leg. "You have not come back empty-handed, brother. The Good Book tells us that a good wife is better than riches."

All fell silent then and looked at Shimin. His hands were hidden beneath the folds of his cloak. He pushed back the cloak slowly, and they saw that his hands were empty. "I do not even have my clay pot," he said sadly.

The father put a loving arm around his youngest son's shoulders. "You have brought yourself back, and that is all that really matters." He smiled at Shimin. "Come, tell us of your travels."

Shimin searched the faces of his brothers and saw no hidden laughter. He took courage and told of the rude, fat man with the impatient customers, the poor potter with the poor customers, and the potter who did inferior work because his customers did not mind being cheated. Finally he managed a grin. "We are lucky to have a father who makes such excellent pots. I was able to sell my bowl and buy food. If he made bowls as poor as many I have seen, I should still be in the city."

Nobody spoke for a long time. Finally the old man said, "Let us talk no more tonight. I want to think about what my sons have learned. Soon it will be Chanukah, and we shall be very busy fashioning menorahs. Haskell and Shimin can teach us the new techniques they have learned. Perhaps Nabar will bake for us. Gershon and I will be learning from you all."

The days of Kislev were passing quickly. Haskell taught his father and brothers how to form beautiful kiddush cups. Shimin purchased a few precious stones from the jeweler and showed his father how to ornament the menorahs. Gershon worked very hard alongside his father. Often he would say to the old man, "Go, visit your friends. I can do the work today." Nabar took over the baking chores and made light, tasty bread and rolls.

Soon more and more people were coming to buy at the potter's shop. Never before in the village had anyone seen such beautiful menorahs, vases, jars, and pots. Often the old man would sit in front of the shop and offer his customers a cup of tea and a hot, fragrant roll.

Life was very pleasant for the father. All his sons were with him, working together and seemingly content. But sometimes he found Nabar dreaming with his eyes open—of the baker's daughter, perhaps? At other times Gershon and Haskell sat silently, their hands suddenly idle. Were they yearning for shops of their own? The wise old man guessed correctly that they would never tell him their thoughts. They knew how lonely he had been during their absence and did not wish to leave him again. But he *wanted* them to follow their dreams. How could he make them understand?

The festivities of Chanukah had begun. Each evening they would light the candles and sing the old songs of freedom. The father especially enjoyed describing the rededication of the Holy Temple in Jerusalem. When he spoke, his sons seemed to smell the incense which was burned, hear the song of the cymbals and harps, and see the fresh loaves that were spread upon the table.

Gershon spoke fiercely. "Ah, Father, I wish I had been there. How I would have fought for liberty and the right to worship God!"

His brothers murmured agreement. The father added, "And after their victory the Jewish people became stronger and more united. They never forgot their fight for freedom and kept the festival of Chanukah alive with songs, stories, and glowing candles."

He smiled at his sons. "And we remember and rededicate ourselves to freedom, too, every year. So do all Jews, no matter where they live."

Shimin nodded thoughtfully. "We are together in our thoughts, even though we are far apart."

On the last night of Chanukah, when all the candles in the menorah were kindled, the old man turned to his sons. "I have been thinking all this month of Kislev about your journeys and what you learned of the world. I feel that each of you has decided what you wish to do with your life, but that you hesitate to say. Am I right?"

The four boys glanced at one another and nodded slowly. Their father continued. "Now you must tell me. Gershon, you are the eldest. You begin."

Gershon hesitated a moment, then said, "I want to return to the village. The people asked me to come back."

"Good. I am pleased that my son wishes to follow my trade."

Haskell spoke. "I can make so many beautiful things now. I'd like to return to the city where there are many people who are interested in the art of making pots and bowls."

"Good. I am happy to know that you wish to follow the trade of your father and your father's father and to improve upon it."

Nabar's face was red, and he could not quite look his father in the eye. "I don't wish to hurt you, Father, but I wish to become a baker...and I want to marry Rachel."

"I am pleased at your decision. I will have a daughter, and that lucky baker...at last he will have a son!"

"It is my turn now," Shimin said softly, "and I suppose I shall disappoint you, Father, but I want to stay here. I like being a potter, and I like the customers we have here in the village."

"Best of all," said the father. "A son to help me in my old age and keep me company...truly I am blessed." He looked at his sons. In spite of their words he saw that they were truly reluctant to leave him. "My sons, you speak of the freedom our forefathers won. Here you have all the freedom you need. Come, do I look like a mother bird who must push her fledglings from the nest?"

The boys all laughed. Their father looked not at all like a mother sparrow. "It is good to hear your laughter," their father said. "Let us go to bed. Tomorrow you may begin to prepare for your departure."

In the days that followed the boys were busy saying good-by to old friends. They visited the tailor for new clothes and the shoemaker for new shoes. Shimin, alone, worked steadily in the shop. He found it hard to make up stories about his customers, for his heart was heavy. Soon his brothers would be going.

The father was very busy, too. On several mornings he arose early while his sons still slept. He worked secretly with clay and a sharp marking stick. Then he baked four oddly shaped clay objects in the oven.

All too soon the day arrived when the three brothers were to depart. After a short, silent breakfast the boys crowded around their father. Their faces were gloomy. Their hearts felt torn in two at the thought of leaving the old man whom they loved so much. Shimin, too, was downcast; he knew he would not see his brothers for a long, long time. The family would never again be the same.

Each boy hugged and kissed his father and brothers good-by. They stood awkwardly in the doorway No one was willing to be the first to leave. Finally Gershon said, "The first time we left we were happy. Now we are all solemn."

Haskell agreed. "The first time we left, we each had a clay pot to remind us of home. We had a little of our home to carry with us."

Shimin's eyes were filled with memories. "That bowl allowed me to return home when I had nothing and no one to help me."

He turned to his father. "Can't they take something along?"

The old man held up his hand. "Yes, I made something for you all just in case saying good-by was very difficult."

He walked to the place where he had hidden the mysterious clay objects and carried them back to his sons. He handed one to each boy.

Each object had four sides and on each side was printed a letter. The bottoms were pointed and the tops were square. Each had a little mound of clay on top for a handle.

"What are they?" the sons chorused.

"I call them *dreidels*. See how they spin?"

"But what are they for?" the boys asked in amazement.

"The dreidels are to remind you of one another. On each side is the first letter of your names. *G* (gimel) for Gershon, *H* (hay) for Haskell, *N* (nun) for Nabar, and *SH* (shin) for Shimin."

Gershon spun his dreidel. It twirled dizzily and fell over with the *G* facing upward. "Father is reminding us that sometimes life will go well, and we'll be on the top. But at other times, we'll be on the bottom."

Haskell nodded. "It spins merrily, but eventually it stops. I think Father wants us to remember that no matter how busy we are, we must rest from our work on the Sabbath as we have always done."

Nabar traced the letters with his finger. "Because Father made it for us during Kislev, I think he wants us to remember the festival of Chanukah and observe it, no matter where we are."

Shimin's words warmed them all. "I think Father wants us to know that we are together, like our initials on the dreidel, even though we are miles apart. During the same days every year we will all light the menorah and spin our dreidel—just as if we were together."

The boys and their father embraced one another again; then the three boys left together. Their hearts were light, for they knew that only distance separated them. They were still a family.

The old man and Shimin waved until Gershon, Haskell, and Nabar were out of sight. Then each went to work molding and pounding the clay. Shimin was silent, content with his choice. The old father was silent and content, too. He was only a simple potter, but he had helped to shape his four boys into four men.

ABOUT THE DREIDEL

The dreidel which the old man made for his sons exists today and is used by both children and adults in a game played at Chanukah.

All players sit in a circle; each is given an equal number of nuts. The nuts are used as a stake in the game, and the winner is the one who manages to acquire the largest number of nuts.

The instructions for the game are on the dreidel itself, which is passed around the circle and spun by each player in turn. The Hebrew letters on the sides of the dreidel tell each player what to do. If he spins a *G*, he gets all the nuts in the middle. An *H* allows him to take half the nuts, the *N* means he takes nothing, and the *SH* means the player must give up a nut. Each player must also contribute a nut to the middle at the beginning of the game and whenever it is cleared by the spinning of a *G* or *H*.

G

H

N

Sh

In the dreidel game lies the logic for this story; for each letter stands for one of the potter's sons. It is as if each son took his spin, and each according to his name was rewarded with the corresponding prize.

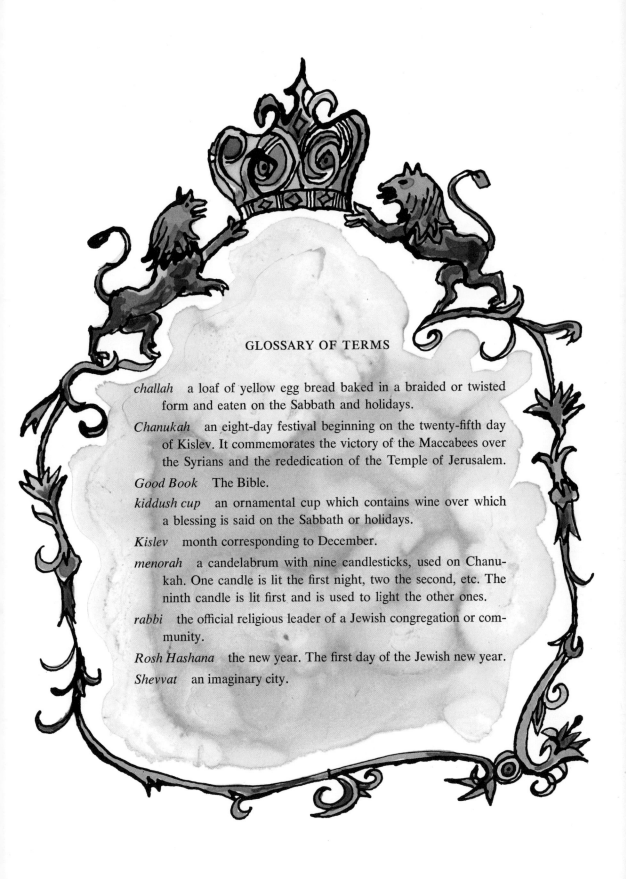

GLOSSARY OF TERMS

challah a loaf of yellow egg bread baked in a braided or twisted form and eaten on the Sabbath and holidays.

Chanukah an eight-day festival beginning on the twenty-fifth day of Kislev. It commemorates the victory of the Maccabees over the Syrians and the rededication of the Temple of Jerusalem.

Good Book The Bible.

kiddush cup an ornamental cup which contains wine over which a blessing is said on the Sabbath or holidays.

Kislev month corresponding to December.

menorah a candelabrum with nine candlesticks, used on Chanukah. One candle is lit the first night, two the second, etc. The ninth candle is lit first and is used to light the other ones.

rabbi the official religious leader of a Jewish congregation or community.

Rosh Hashana the new year. The first day of the Jewish new year.

Shevvat an imaginary city.

Sharlya Gold was born in Los Angeles, California, attended schools in San Bernardino Valley, and received a B.A. degree from the University of California at Berkeley. Though this is her first book, she has "always written" and has previously contributed articles to a variety of children's and instructional magazines. Mrs. Gold now lives in Rialto, California, with her husband and four daughters.

Jules Maidoff was born in New York and received his B.A. and M.A. degrees at Cooper Union. After graduation he continued his studies in Italy with a Fulbright Scholarship. He has exhibited in Italy and New York and is represented in many museums and private collections. Mr. Maidoff now lives in New York with his wife and five children and has his own studio called Asterisk Associates.